DINOSAUR RESCUE

KYLE MEWBURN & DONOVAN BIXLEY

SALTO-SCAREDYPUS

SCHOLASTIC

AUCKLAND SYDNEY NEW YORK LONDON TORONTO
MEXICO CITY NEW DELHI HONG KONG BUENOS AIRES

Arg's Valley

1. Pterosaur Cliffs
2. Lava Mountain
3. Bog
4. Slimepot Swamp
5. Big Bone Lake
6. Village Fire Pit
7. Way to Nn-Grrrdy Valley
8. Arg's Village
9. Stinkooze Pit

Nn-Grrrdy
a tribe
of criminal
cavemen

Hng
Arg's big
sister

Arg's mother

Arg's father

The author would like to point out he doesn't really believe Neanderthals and dinosaurs lived at the same time. He certainly didn't see any dinosaurs when he visited the Stone Age in his time machine while researching this book.

First published in 2013 by Scholastic New Zealand Limited
Private Bag 94407, Botany, Auckland 2163, New Zealand

Scholastic Australia Pty Limited
PO Box 579, Gosford, NSW 2250, Australia

Text © Kyle Mewburn, 2013
Illustrations © Donovan Bixley, 2013

ISBN 978-1-77543-121-3

National Library of New Zealand Cataloguing-in-Publication Data

Mewburn, Kyle.
Salto-scaredypus / by Kyle Mewburn ; illustrated by Donovan Bixley.
(Dinosaur rescue)
ISBN 978-1-77543-121-3
[1. Neanderthals—Fiction. 2. Dinosaurs—Fiction. 3. Humorous stories.]
I. Bixley, Donovan. II. Title. III. Series: Mewburn, Kyle. Dinosaur rescue.
NZ823.2—dc 23

12 11 10 9 8 7 6 5 4 3 2 1   3 4 5 6 7 8 9 / 1

Publishing team: Diana Murray, Penny Scown and Frith Hughes
Design and layup by Donovan Bixley
Typeset in Berkeley Oldstyle
Printed in China by RR Donnelley

Scholastic New Zealand's policy, in association with RR Donnelley, is to use papers that are renewable and made efficiently from wood grown in sustainable forests, so as to minimise its environmental footprint.

For Ollie and Rhys. Two clever Matamata cave boys – K.M.

For Hanna, a true ~~poo~~ *blue fan* – D.B.

RRrrr

A Guide to the Nn-Grrrdy
How to spot a Neanderthal ne'er-do-well

Haircuts
Nn-Grrrdy cut their hair with sharp flints to look respectable from the front, but they are ALL party at the back

Shifty Eyes
Always looking for something to steal

Tattoos
Men use sharp flints to carve 'stink lines' in their arms

Light Fingers
Long, nimble hands show Nn-Grrrdy are closely related to monkeys

Clothing
Threadbare dinosaur skins are itchy and cold

Sharp Flints
Nn-Grrrdy trade in sharp stones, saving the biggest as their own weapons of mass destruction

Sneaky Feet
Nn-Grrrdy have heavily padded feet from walking on hard rocks. This helps them to sneak quietly

CHAPTER ONE

Arg's village was a whirlwind of activity. The Nn-Grrrdy tribe was coming to barter and would be there in no time. But there were still heaps of things that needed to be done before they arrived …

Like hiding all the best mammoth skins … and the dried brontosaurus poo supply … and the spare flints … and basically everything else Arg's tribe owned. The Nn-Grrrdy were very greedy. If they saw how much stuff Arg's tribe had, they would drive a much harder bargain. They were also very sneaky. If you left anything lying around, an Nn-Grrrdy was sure to steal it.

While the women ran around hiding everything, the hunters all made sure their spears were sharp and ready for combat. The Nn-Grrrdy were very aggressive.

They would just as soon kill you and steal your stuff as barter. Arg's tribe couldn't let their guard down for a second.

The Nn-Grrrdy didn't really like bartering. But the cold time was coming soon and they needed mammoth

Nn-Grrrdy Fashion Experiments with Dinosaur Skin

Ankylosaur Armour
Take on any challenge with this 300kg protective cloak

T-rex Tutu
Dance the night away in this delightful dress

hides to keep warm. There weren't any mammoths in their valley. It was too steep and rocky. There were plenty of dinosaurs, but dinosaur skins didn't keep you warm. They just made you itchy. They were very rough and terribly stiff.

Brontosaur
Body Sock
This elegant item
is very slimming
and made from
brontosaurus neck

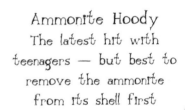

Ammonite Hoody
The latest hit with
teenagers — but best to
remove the ammonite
from its shell first

Stegosaur Sundress
and Pterasaur Parasol
Now you can go in the
sun AND be fashionable at
the same time

Nobody liked bartering with the Nn-Grrrdy either. They were not very pleasant. They always criticised and complained. The only tribe less pleasant than the Nn-Grrrdy were the Grogllgrox. But the Nn-Grrrdy had one thing every tribe wanted – sharp flints. The Nn-Grrrdy's valley had the sharpest flint stones anywhere.

Arg raced around the clearing, searching for a safe place to hide his best stuff. His arms were loaded with his spare sabre-toothed tiger coat, his weird rock collection and his painting poos, plus loads of polished bone shards and colourful  fragments of shell. (Okay, so the bone shards and shell fragments weren't really his *best* stuff, but he'd taken ages to collect them. They weren't just any old bone shards – each one of them looked like something else. One looked like his mum. Another one looked like a farting allosaurus. And one looked like his sister, Hng, after she'd been melted by a volcano. That was his favourite. And the colourful shell fragments were just so ... well, *colourful*.)

The tribe was slowly gathering around the fire pit to welcome the Nn-Grrrdy. Actually it was more a show of force than a welcome. Everyone was very nervous. The Nn-Grrrdy might try to sneak up and ambush them if they weren't on their toes.

Arg's dad was stacking all the mammoth hides the tribe wanted to barter near the fire pit. Most of the hides were from before the last cold times. Some of

them were very thin and worn. Others had big holes
in them where the mammoth got speared. All the
best hides were hidden away so the Nn-Grrrdy
wouldn't see them. Arg's tribe would need the
warmest hides for themselves if they wanted to
survive the next cold time.

When the Nn-Grrrdy arrived, there would be a
huge feast. Arg's mum had roasted two iguanodons
specially. They were charred on the outside and
almost raw in the middle – just like the Nn-Grrrdy
liked them.

There was also a bronto-skull full of fermented cycad sap. Arg's dad said the Nn-Grrrdy were much more pleasant after they drank some cycad sap. Except for one time when they drank so much cycad sap that they thought the mammoth hides were alive and ...

But that's another story.

Hng was sitting by the fire with an evil smile on her face. Arg didn't know why she was there. All the other girls were hiding in case the Nn-Grrrdy wanted to barter *them*. Arg wouldn't mind if his dad bartered Hng for some flints. Though he'd feel a bit sorry for the Nn-Grrrdy.

Arg would have to be very careful Hng didn't see where he hid his stuff or she was sure to tell someone.

All the normal hiding places – under rocks, in trees, behind bushes – were full already. Most of the stuff wasn't hidden very well. Stone Age people weren't very good at hiding.

One time, Arg invented a new game called 'Hide and Find'. He thought it would be fun if someone hid and the other person had to find them. But it was a disaster!

When it was Shlok's turn to hide, he just stood somewhere and covered his face with a leaf. He thought if he couldn't see Arg, then Arg couldn't see him either.

And as soon as Arg hid, Shlok forgot they were playing a game. When he heard something moving behind a cycad, he thought it might be something to eat. So he threw his spear at it.

He was very surprised when he went to retrieve it and discovered Arg pinned to a tree.

Sometimes it was very hard having a bigger brain than everyone else, Arg thought.

A loud shout echoed
from high up on the cliff.
The lookout had spotted
the Nn-Grrrdy barter party.
They were nearly there.

Arg's head whipped one way then the other. He
had to find somewhere to stash all his stuff. And fast.

At the edge of the clearing he spotted a small hole
at the base of a big cycad. It looked like some kind of
burrow. Arg raced over. There was no time to wonder

what kind of dinosaur had made the hole.
He quickly dumped everything on the ground
and started shoving his stuff inside.

He had a LOT of stuff.

Sometimes he thought having so much stuff was not a good idea. Imagine if *everyone* wanted lots of stuff! There wouldn't be enough stuff to go around.

A brief glimpse into the future of Stuff

Is there really anything to fear from Stuff?

Give stuff!

STONE AGE

People would always be fighting and having wars and stealing each other's stuff. You'd have to be pretty dumb to let that happen.

The lookout gave another call.

Arg shot a quick glance back over his shoulder. Oh no! The first Nn-Grrrdy was already strolling into the clearing. Arg's spare sabre-toothed tiger coat was still spread across the ground like a blanket. If he didn't hurry, the Nn-Grrrdy would be sure to see it.

Arg scrambled to his feet and started stomping on his coat. "Get *in* there," he muttered. But it wouldn't

budge. The burrow was full to the brim.

With a cry of frustration, Arg leapt in the air. His feet plunged down, into the centre of the hole. *Ha! Take that!* Arg cheered as his coat slurped further down the burrow.

His jubilation only lasted a single breath.

Arg felt a light tremble as the ground gave way beneath his feet. Then the hole swallowed him whole.

Bartering for Beginners

Bartering is a very complicated business. In the wild, things don't have prices on them like in supermarkets. So buyers and sellers have to argue until they agree on a price. The sellers try to get as much as they can, while the buyers try to pay as little as possible.

The problem is, prices can change a lot depending on circumstances. If you were stuck on a glacier, you'd probably give anything for a mammoth hide. But if someone offered the exact same mammoth hide when you were lying on a warm, sunny beach, you wouldn't give much at all.

During mammoth plagues you couldn't ask much for a mammoth hide either. But if you killed the last mammoth in the world, people would give you almost anything for its hide.

You might get more for an unusually striped or polka-dot mammoth hide, too. Especially if everyone in the neighbouring village already had one, or a famous hunter started wearing one.

For a while people tried to trade using other things like shells or barley or donkeys. But it was even more confusing trying to figure out how many shells a bag of barley was worth. And donkeys couldn't fit in your pocket.

HEE HAW

That's why people invented money. The first money was invented by the Lydians around 600 BC. The Lydians lived in Anatolia, which is part of Turkey (the country, not the bird).

Money made things easier, but it didn't really make it any less complicated because money doesn't have any real value. In fact, most of the world's money doesn't even exist. (But if everyone *knew* that, nobody would go to work to earn money to buy stuff because everyone would share everything and people could spend all day playing and having fun instead of working or doing homework or other boring stuff like that. So whatever you do, *DON'T* tell anyone!)

MAMMOTH HUNTER PRODUCTIONS
PRESENTS...

THE
MAMMOTH HUNTER'S
GUIDE TO
HUNTING MAMMOTHS*

Join Crik-ee,
the world's** BEST
mammoth hunter,
on the
MOST
EXTREME
HUNTING
adventure
ever!***

Discover why mammoths are one of the most dangerous animals to hunt! Watch as Crik-ee turns a herd of stampeding mammoths into a mountain of steak, a pile of winter hides and a clatter of tusks in time for the next barter.

COMING SOON, TO A CAVE NEAR YOU!

* Available on VBR (Very Big Rocks) and WP3 (Wall Painting version 3)
** For Neanderthals, 'the world' means only the surrounding valleys, or the distance a hunting party can walk without getting lost.
*** Neanderthals have very short memories, so 'ever' doesn't really mean, you know, like FOREVER ever. Hmmm, actually 'ever' NEVER really means FOREVER ever, does it? So kindly forget this whole point.

CHAPTER TWO

Ah-h-h-h-h-h-h-h-h-h-h-h

Arg's scream spiralled up the chimney hole then burst into the clearing. The arriving band of Nn-Grrrdy were so shocked, they bolted upright until their knuckles were no longer scraping along the ground. (The Nn-Grrrdy were not very

advanced. Some Neanderthals said they were just talking monkeys really. Neanderthals can be very cruel.) They gripped their spears tightly and glanced nervously around. Was it an ambush? Or an attack by a strange creature they'd never seen before?

Across the clearing, the hunters in Arg's tribe were doing exactly the same thing. Nobody had heard such a strange, echoing wail before.

The two tribes stood poised on opposite sides of the clearing. Would they have to fight or flee? Nobody knew yet. It all depended on what happened next.

Ah-h-h-h-h-h-h-h-h-h-h -h-h-h-h!

Finally, the sound faded. Hunters from both tribes
breathed enormous sighs of relief ... until they
remembered the other tribe was watching them.
As their faces turned red with embarrassment,
they puffed up their chests and tried to look

tough. They bared their teeth and snarled at each other across the clearing.

When they noticed the other tribe was doing exactly the same thing, they all burst out laughing.

It was the perfect start to a bartering.

Meanwhile ...

Arg plummeted down the hole like a muddy meteorite. Darkness engulfed him. It was so dark he couldn't see his own nose. Which was kind of lucky, really. He wasn't sure he wanted to see what the soft, squishy things were that squelched against his skin as he flashed past.

Down, down he zapped.

Faster and faster.

If the whole world really was on the back of a giant turtle like everyone thought, he'd soon go sliding right off. How would he ever get home then?

Slowly, the darkness began to dissolve. Arg saw that the burrow was lined with tree roots as fine as hair. Giant worms were weaving

amongst the roots like maggots in a rotting carcass. Worm heads and tails lashed Arg's face as he swooshed past. His bum left a smear of squashed worms in its wake.

As Arg swept around a corner, his eyes flew open. Up ahead, the tunnel ended in a jagged circle of light. He couldn't see what was on the other side. The hole could spit him out anywhere. He might be shot into a bubbling volcano. Or dumped into a lava lake. Or sent tumbling right off the bottom of the world. Or ...

Arg sighed. Sometimes his big brain wasn't much help at all.

Arg dug his heels deeply into the mud and stuck out his elbows like archaeopteryx wings.

His hands snatched at root hairs. But the tunnel was slippery as ice. Nothing could slow him down.

When a nosy worm stuck its head out of the mud, Arg grabbed it.

The worm stretched longer ...
and longer.
Arg got slower ... and slower.
It was working! It was ...
The worm's head pulled off
with a loud,
squelchy *plop!*

Arg shot out of the tunnel into empty space. He frantically glanced around, looking for something to grab on to. The tunnel was halfway up the wall of a vast underground cavern.

High above, Arg glimpsed a ceiling covered with countless roosting bats. Far below, he saw his spare sabre-toothed tiger coat and the rest of his stuff scattered over a grey-and-white speckled floor.

In between was nothing but warm, stinky air.

"Ah-h-h-h-h-h-h-h-h-h-h-h-h-h!"

Arg's scream ricocheted up the cavern walls and bounced along the ceiling. Waves of frightened bats were swept into the air like shrieking dust balls. They dived and swirled around Arg in thick clouds. Their high-pitched squeaks sent shivers up Arg's spine. One of them was sure to smash into him any second. He couldn't bear to watch.

But as soon as Arg scrunched up his eyes, the
terrible fate awaiting him began playing in his head.
He imagined his broken body being sucked dry by
swarms of blood-sucking bats. Then he would become
a half-bat/half-boy creature and sneak into his village
at night to suck their blood and turn everyone else
into bat people. And before long he'd start wearing
a black costume with pointy bat ears and a bat belt
and drive around in a bat-shaped wagon fighting
evil-doers and ... wait a second, that was a different
story, wasn't it?

Oh well, never mind. It didn't really matter what fate awaited him. He just knew it would be terrible.

The ground wasn't hard after all. That was good.

In fact … it wasn't really what you'd call 'ground'. The whole cavern floor was a massive mound of bat droppings. Which wasn't quite so good.

Poo filled Arg's nose, stung his eyes and prickled

his skin as he submerged into the stinky mess. He held his breath and clamped his mouth shut. He had to get out of there. And fast! He only had a few seconds – tops – before he'd have to breathe again. If that happened, he was a goner.

Arg frantically kicked his legs and thrashed his arms until his head broke through the surface. He took a rasping breath, then part-swam, part-crawled, part-dragged himself through the squelchy poo.

Closer to the edge, the surface began to harden.

Arg hauled himself out and stood. By the time he'd scraped himself clean ... well, sort of clean … the bats had returned to their roosts in the shadows of the ceiling. Apart from the sound of snuffling bat snores and fidgety wings being refolded, the cavern was eerily silent. It was spookily gloomy, too.

A single sliver of sunshine poured through a narrow crack in the wall. It bathed the wall behind Arg in pale light. But the rest of the cavern was thick with shadows. They seemed to swirl around like fog.

sniff
sniff

Now what? Arg wondered.

There had to be another way out. There was no way all those bats scrambled through that narrow crack every dusk. They'd have to line up for hours.

But he was reluctant to move. Who knew what was lurking in the gloom. What if the cavern was like a maze and he took a wrong turn? He could spend his whole life wandering through dead-end corridors.

As his gaze swept around the cavern, he felt the faint trace of a breeze against one cheek. Arg sniffed the air. It was fresh, all right. And it wasn't sneaking through the crack in the wall, either. It was coming from the other side of the darkness.

Arg squared his shoulders, took a deep breath, then set off.

After three steps he spun around and scuttled back up the mound. He retrieved his spare sabre-toothed tiger coat and his favourite bone shard (the one that looked like Hng after she'd been melted in a volcano), then set off once more – pausing to sniff the breeze with every step.

Amazing facts about fat bats on mats patting flat rats with hats

Bats are amazing. For a start, they are the only flying mammals in the world (unless you count pilots). There are over 1,200 different types of bat. In fact, 20% of all mammals are bats. (20.0000000000000001% if you count Batman.)

Most bats eat insects. A LOT of insects. If there were no bats, the world would soon be knee-deep in insects. It would be very difficult to play golf (or any sport, really … except maybe cricket – haha!) and picnics would be no fun at all. Most other bats eat fruit. A few eat tiny animals or even fish. Vampires are the only bats that drink blood. But for some reason they're usually the first bat people think of.

In most western countries, bats are linked to witchcraft and black magic. (Except for baseball bats, which have no link to witchcraft or black magic at all. Though they *are* very useful for knocking out witches and zombies.)

In places like China and Poland, however, bats are symbols of happiness and good luck.

In many countries the word for bat means 'flying mouse' (e.g. in Germany, it's *Fledermaus*). But bats are not related to mice or other rodents at all. In fact, the bat's closest relatives are alpacas, hippopotamuses and dolphins. If a bat had a birthday party and invited all its relatives, it would be a very weird party and it would get some very strange presents!

Most bats are nocturnal. They come out to hunt and feed at night. They find their way by sending out ultrasonic sounds. When the sounds hit objects they bounce back, creating ultrasonic images like a radar.

Bats are not blind. But if they were people, they'd have to wear very thick glasses. They have a very good sense of smell and hearing though. So it wouldn't be much fun playing Hide and Find with a bat.

Bats are especially amazing compared to oranges. Nothing rhymes with orange.

CHAPTER THREE

At the end of the cavern, Arg found a dark hole punched through the wall. The sound of running water became louder as he clambered through. For a second he thought he'd found the exit.

But it was just another cavern, slightly smaller than the first. The second cavern was cold and damp. A narrow stream trickled between knobbly stalagmites before disappearing down a crack in the floor. Stalactites clung to the ceiling like fangs, drooling droplets of icy water down Arg's neck. But at least there were no bats.

He spotted another large hole halfway up the far wall, bathed in ghostly light. Arg's heart quickened. It was definitely getting lighter, which meant he was definitely heading the right way.

Arg's footsteps sounded like wet slaps on the rocky ground as he hurried over. He heaved himself up the wall. The breeze strengthened as it funnelled through the hole. The unmistakable smell of the jungle filled Arg's nose and brought a smile to his face. Outside wasn't too far away now.

The next cavern was like a different world. It was lighter, for a start. Sunlight streamed through several holes in the ceiling. Everything was covered with moss and fungus and lichens and all sorts of plant life. Arg didn't really understand why there were no plants at all in the other caverns. Maybe the bats ate them all?

He wasn't about to hang around to try and solve *that* mystery.

The wall was way too slippery to climb down. So Arg gripped the edge of the hole and gently lowered himself. When he was hanging with his face pressed flat against the moss, he took a deep breath … then let go.

He slid down the wall and landed with a dull thud. The floor was so thick with moss, it didn't hurt at all.

A crooked grin twisted Arg's lips …

Boing

50

then froze as a cold shiver of dread shot up his spine.
The cavern floor was littered with gnawed and
splintered bones. Something was using the cavern
as its den. He had to get out of there fast, before it
came home.

His gaze swept one way, then the other.

A large hole directly ahead promised an easy exit.
Even though it was half covered by a rockslide, Arg
didn't think it would be too hard to clamber up
there. There was only one problem. An exit was also
an entrance. Whatever lived here could come back
anytime. It might even be snoozing in the sun, just
outside. It wouldn't be very happy to see a cave boy
trying to escape from its lair.

There had to be a safer escape route.

Long strands of moss drooped down from the
ceiling like ropes. They wouldn't be too hard to
climb. But were they strong enough to hold
a cave boy? If the moss rope broke before
he reached the top it was a long way
down. He wasn't sure the floor was
soft enough to cushion his fall
from that height.

There was another large hole to his left. It wasn't too high up. There was even a dead tree trunk leaning against the wall directly below it. Almost as if someone had put it there to use as a ladder. Even though the trunk ended a spear-length short, he was sure he'd manage to get out somehow.

He scurried over. But as soon as he stepped onto the bottom branch of the trunk, it began to wobble and sway. It wasn't very stable at all.

He slumped back to the ground with a sigh.

"Eek! Eek!"

Arg spun around. His legs were coiled like cycad shoots, ready to spring into action. There was something moving in the shadows on the far side of the cavern.

A saltopus strutted into the light. Arg gave a nervous laugh. "Ha! Boy you gave me a fright."

Saltopuses were too small to be dangerous. They were real scaredy-saurs, too. That's why they were such fast runners.

"You better get out of here quick," said Arg. "If the beast that lives here comes home, you'll be dinner."

Saltopus
The light-footed scavenger

1. Saltopus means 'hopping foot'. It is not related to the octopus (meaning 'eight-footed')
2. Bones are hollow like pterasaur bones, making it light and swift
3. Small teeth are useful for scavenging meat
4. Saltopus is usually a happy dinosaur, not like its cousin – the sourpus
5. Size compared to Arg: their small size makes people THINK they are scaredy-saurs like microceratops, but be careful, never insult a saltopus or it will result in an assault

SOURPUS

The saltopus strutted closer. It gave Arg a toothy smile. Arg started to smile back, but a thought intruded. How did the saltopus get in there? Saltopuses were very fast but they weren't very agile. There was no way it could clamber down the rockslide. And it certainly didn't climb down a mossy rope or a wobbly tree trunk either. Which meant there had to be another way in!

Arg's eyes narrowed. The cavern walls looked solid enough. At least the ones he could see clearly were. If there was another exit, it must be hidden somewhere in the shadows on the other side.

He only got five steps before the saltopus cut him off. It stood in his way and bared its teeth. "Eek! Eek!" it screeched.

"Don't be scared," soothed Arg. "If I find a way out, I'll come back to get you. Okay?"

He tried to dodge past but the saltopus was too quick.

"Eeeek! Eeeeek!" it screeched, louder than before.

"Shoo, you stupid saltopus," said Arg. He swung

his foot and gave the saltopus a gentle kick. "If you don't get out of the way now, I'll ... *Owww!*" Arg squealed as the saltopus chomped his toe.

"Hey!" Arg yanked his throbbing toe from the saltopus's jaws. "You're supposed to be a scavenger, not a predator!"

The saltopus bared its fangs then lunged at Arg's other foot.

Arg hopped away just in time. The saltopus circled round. "Eeek! Eeek!" it screeched again.

"Eek! Eek!"

Arg bolted upright. Every muscle in his body began to quiver. That wasn't an echo.

Another saltopus strutted out of the shadow.

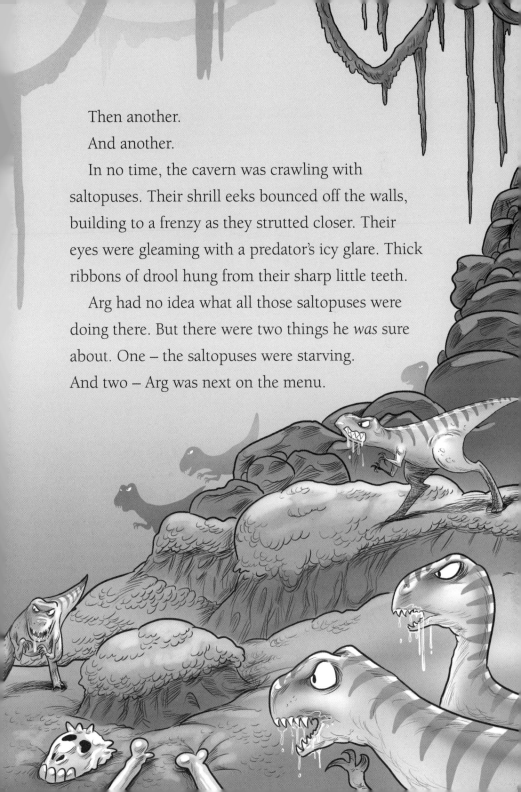

Then another.

And another.

In no time, the cavern was crawling with saltopuses. Their shrill eeks bounced off the walls, building to a frenzy as they strutted closer. Their eyes were gleaming with a predator's icy glare. Thick ribbons of drool hung from their sharp little teeth.

Arg had no idea what all those saltopuses were doing there. But there were two things he *was* sure about. One – the saltopuses were starving. And two – Arg was next on the menu.

THE MAMMOTH HUNTER'S GUIDE TO HUNTING MAMMOTHS

EPISODE ONE
MAMMOTH HUNTING DOs & DON'Ts

Mammoths are one of the most dangerous animals to hunt. So there are a few important things you need to remember:

1 Mammoths are very big and very fast. No hunter can outrun a mammoth. Especially not an angry mammoth with a spear stuck in its bum. You should NEVER approach a mammoth from in front. If you DO approach a mammoth from in front, make sure you have a slow friend beside you. If you DON'T have a slow friend, make sure you are NOT wearing anything red. If you ARE wearing something red ... well, good luck!

2 Mammoths have very long, very pointy tusks. When hunting in a group, never EVER line up behind each other when a mammoth charges.

3 Mammoths are very clever. If you don't stay on your toes, they will out-manoeuvre you and pop up in the most unexpected places.

4 Mammoths have very long memories. If you injure a mammoth, you must finish it off. No matter how long it takes. This is not only the humane thing to do, it is the intelligent thing to do. If you DON'T kill the mammoth, one day when you least expect it, you will discover the mammoth has come for revenge.

5 The thing that makes mammoths even more dangerous than spinosaurs is that mammoths live in herds. It can be very difficult to separate a victim from the rest of the herd. That's why most hunters don't try to spear mammoths, but chase the whole herd over a cliff ... after first making sure there's nobody standing at the bottom of the cliff.

6 Mammoth hunting requires teamwork. It's a good idea for every hunter to wear something so they can be easily seen. More hunters get killed by other hunters than by mammoths. It is NOT a good idea to try and sneak up on a mammoth herd by disguising yourself as a mammoth.

So, that's all for this moon. Next moon we'll be looking at the 267 ways a mammoth can kill you. Hope you're still alive to join us. Until then, happy hunting!

CHAPTER FOUR

Arg bolted for the tree trunk. The saltopuses were in hot pursuit. He leapt onto the first branch. But he was a fraction too slow. A saltopus leapt up and snatched the tail of Arg's coat.

"Get off me!" squealed Arg.

He kicked out and tried to hoist himself higher. Two more saltopuses latched onto his coat. A third quickly joined in. Then another – and another. Arg gripped the branch tightly as the saltopuses began to violently tug and yank on his coat, trying to pull him loose. With each tug the tree trunk wobbled and shifted dangerously. Any second now it was going to topple over.

Arg strained to heave himself higher. Saltopuses weren't climbers. If he could just scramble out of reach ...

But the saltopuses weren't about to let a meal escape. Their excited eeks were growing louder with every tug, while Arg's arms were getting weaker and weaker. If he didn't think of something quickly, he was a goner.

Suddenly, a series of loud, piercing shrieks echoed through the cavern. The saltopuses halted their frenzied assault and cocked their heads to listen. The shrieks got louder. Tiny avalanches of pebbles and dirt tumbled down the cavern wall. Something

was approaching the hole directly above Arg.

He craned his neck to get a glimpse of the new peril. But all he got was a face full of dust.

The shrieks got louder and more urgent. One by one, the saltopuses let go of Arg's coat and shuffled backwards. They crowded together and peered up at the hole.

When a stygimoloch leapt through into thin air, Arg could only blink with bewilderment. He didn't know stygimolochs could fly.

The stygimoloch let out a terrified shriek. It wasn't flying. It was falling.

It didn't make sense. Why would a stygimoloch jump into a cavern full of ravaging saltopuses? It would be certain death. And how did the saltopuses guess something was about to happen?

As Arg twisted around to follow the stygimoloch's descent, the sun splashed through the hole and painted a shadow on the opposite wall. Arg almost cheered.

Aha! There was the answer! Someone was up there. He was saved!

The stygimoloch hit the cavern floor with a sickening THUD! Loud enough to make Arg grimace. He was sure it was dead but it bounded upright and shook its head. When it noticed the saltopuses closing in, it gave a feeble squeal of fear and spun in a tight circle, looking for a gap in the ring of snarling saltopuses. But there was no escape.

As the stygimoloch twisted round, several saltopuses lunged and latched onto its back legs. The stygimoloch bucked and kicked but the saltopuses held on grimly. In desperation the stygimoloch twisted round and tried to butt a saltopus loose with its head. But all it did was expose its neck to another wave of attack.

CRACK!

The stygimoloch's squeals
turned into shrieks of pain as
fangs punctured its tough skin.

Arg had to admit it was a
clever rescue plan to toss the
stygimoloch into the cavern to distract
the saltopuses. He couldn't quite figure out how his
rescuer knew Arg was in there, or how he managed
to catch a stygimoloch so quickly. He'd have plenty
of time to ask those questions later.

Arg couldn't bear to watch the slaughter. There
was nothing he could do to help the stygimoloch
anyway. And if he didn't make the most of the
diversion, he'd be the saltopuses' dessert.

He hurriedly clambered up the tree trunk, out of
harm's way. It was hard to keep his balance. The
trunk rocked and wobbled with each step. One false
move and it would go crashing to the floor.

Arg didn't glance down until he reached the top.
When he did, his stomach lurched. What a terrible
way to go!

Cringing, Arg carefully peered upwards. He glimpsed the top of a head craning over the edge. But there was no sign of a helpful hand ... or a rope ... or anything. Whoever was standing up there was too busy watching the saltopuses devouring the stygimoloch to help Arg.

"Hey!" shouted Arg. "You haven't rescued me yet!"

The figure jerked away from the hole as if Arg's voice was a total surprise. Arg frowned. Maybe his rescuer didn't have a very good memory. Or maybe he wasn't as clever as Arg imagined.

The figure slowly returned. A head poked over the edge of the hole and looked down. It was a young cave boy about Arg's age.

Arg offered his best smile. The boy replied with a dark frown. He didn't look as frowny as most Neanderthals, but he didn't look as though he had a brain as big as Arg's either.

"Thanks for rescuing me," said Arg, "but I can't quite get up there by myself. So you wouldn't mind giving me a hand up, would you?"

Arg carefully stretched one hand up as far it would go.

The boy just stared at Arg's hand. His frown deepened.

Arg rolled his eyes. Boy, how dumb could the cave boy be?

Finally, the cave boy smiled. It wasn't the friendliest smile. In fact, it kind of reminded Arg of Hng's smile. But right now he couldn't afford to be fussy.

"Me want coat," the boy said, pointing at the spare sabre-toothed tiger coat draped over Arg's neck.

Now it was Arg's turn to frown. The boy wasn't trying to barter, was he? That wouldn't be a very nice thing to do. But why else would he want Arg's coat? Unless ... unless he was going to use it as a rope to hoist Arg out! That was a clever idea. It was exactly what Arg would do.

"Good idea!" Arg encouraged.

With one hand clinging tightly to the tree trunk, he gently teased his coat from his shoulders then swung it upwards. The boy snatched the other end.

"Right!" said Arg. "I'll count to three and then ..."

The boy gave the coat a
massive tug. It caught Arg
completely off guard. "Hey!"
yelled Arg, as the coat was
whipped from his hand.
The boy leaned over the edge
and gave Arg an evil grin.

"Hey!" yelled Arg again. "You can't just
leave me here!"

The boy shrugged, then withdrew.

Arg was furious. He wasn't going to let him get
away with that. When he got his hands on that
dumb cave boy he'd …

He planted his foot on the
very top of the tree trunk,
then launched himself up
the cavern wall.

BAD MOVE!

He managed to hook his fingers on the edge of the hole. But it quickly crumbled, leaving him with a handful of dust.

As he slid back down the wall, he grabbed the tree trunk. It wobbled once …

then toppled sideways.

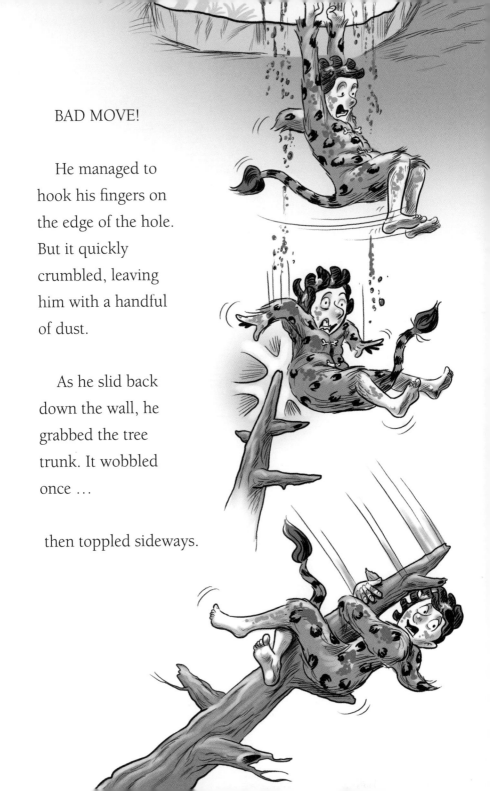

CHAPTER FIVE

Arg couldn't decide which was worse – being
smashed to smithereens by a huge tree trunk or
eaten alive by saltopuses. Actually, he *could* decide.
In fact, it was a very easy decision. Nothing could be
more terrible than being eaten alive. Unfortunately,
it wasn't his decision to make.

As the tree trunk toppled, Arg
was tossed free. He sailed through
the air then landed with a heavy

thump on a thick pile of moss. The trunk smashed
into the base of the rockslide at the cave entrance.
So he didn't get crushed after all. He didn't even get
knocked unconscious. He just had the wind
knocked out of him.

Great, he thought as he lay wheezing on the
ground. *Now I'm going to be totally awake when I get
eaten alive by the saltopuses.*

He wished his T-rex friend Skeet was there. He'd
show those stupid saltopuses what a real carnivore
was like.

The first saltopuses were abandoning the stygimoloch feast. Their jaws were drenched with blood. One of them was bound to notice Arg any second. And when they did ...

A cracking, rumbling sound echoed through the cavern. The saltopuses jerked to attention and began looking nervously around.

What now? thought Arg.

A large boulder tumbled down from the top of the rockslide. Arg leapt to his feet and dived out of the way, just in time. It rolled through the cavern, sending saltopuses scuttling for safety.

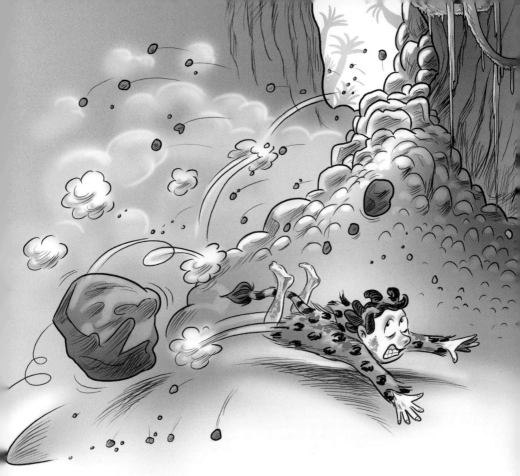

A second boulder wasn't far behind. The tree trunk had shaken the rockslide enough to unsettle it. Now it was crumbling completely.

Arg clambered onto a narrow ledge and held on grimly as the boulders rumbled past. Dust clouds plumed into the air. He held his breath and shut his eyes until the rumbling faded.

When the dust finally settled, the cavern entrance
was clear. Sunlight and fresh air poured in. Arg
stumbled towards the outside world,
spitting out mouthfuls of dust.
He stood at the cavern
mouth and breathed in
huge gulps of air. He was
relieved to realise that
he recognised the
surrounding cliffs.
He hadn't fallen out the
other end of the world.

In fact, he wasn't too far from home. If he hurried, he might even be in time for the feast and …

"Eeeeek!"

Arg slowly turned. The saltopuses had discovered the exit too. They didn't look pleased to be free; they just looked hungry.

Arg backed away.

"You don't have to eat *me* now," he said, holding his hands up to show he meant no harm.

"There's plenty of tastier things around."

The saltopuses stalked closer. Most of them were still licking blood off their lips.

Arg knew he couldn't outrun a healthy saltopus. But these saltopuses didn't look that healthy. They'd obviously been trapped in that cavern a long time, relying on the mystery cave boy to feed them. There was only one way to find out just how unhealthy they were.

Arg spun away and bolted for home with a whole horde of hungry saltopuses snapping at his heels.

Meanwhile ...

The bartering was going very smoothly. At least Arg's dad thought so.

A reasonable number of mammoth hides were now piled up on the Nn-Grrrdy side of the fire, while an impressive stack of flint stones had been swapped over to the other side. It seemed like a fair and reasonable exchange.

The Nn-Grrrdy had eaten the charred iguanodons and drunk some fermented cycad sap without a single complaint or nasty comment. That should have made Arg's dad nervous. The Nn-Grrrdy were *always* complaining. But Arg's dad had drunk a little too much cycad sap himself. He was feeling very happy with his day. The Nn-Grrrdy weren't so horrible after all.

In fact, he was feeling so happy, he decided to throw in an extra mammoth hide. Just to be nice.

But as he struggled to his feet, the Nn-Grrrdy
leapt up and grabbed their spears. Arg's tribe was
caught completely by surprise. All the hunters were
surrounded before they knew what was happening.

Everyone was quickly herded together and forced
to watch silently while the Nn-Grrrdy gathered up

all the hides *and* all the flint stones and anything else they could find. There was nothing Arg's tribe could do to stop them taking everything.

The Nn-Grrrdy were just preparing to leave when the jungle started to shiver. Then a scream shattered the uneasy silence.

"Da-a-a-a-a-a-a-a-ad!"

Arg burst into the clearing. Rivers of sweat
rolled down his dust-covered face, painting strange,
reddish stripes.

The Nn-Grrrdy chief grinned. It was just a boy. They might as well take him along as well. They needed a few more slaves. This was turning out to be a very good day. When they got back to camp, he'd–

A wave of saltopuses poured out of the jungle.

The Nn-Grrrdy just stood there, frowning. Their jaws swung open even more than normal. They didn't know what was happening. Everyone knew saltopuses were scaredy-saurs. Except that *these* saltopuses didn't look scared at all. With gleaming eyes and blood-stained jaws, they looked rather dangerous. But there was no way a brave hunter would ever run away from a silly saltopus. It would be way too embarrassing!

Arg's dad didn't really know what was happening either. He just knew Arg was in trouble. That was enough to make him spring into action.

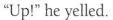

"Up!" he yelled.

Everyone in Arg's tribe obeyed instantly. Even the hunters weren't very keen to face these saltopuses. Especially not without their spears. They started clambering up the cliff to safety.

Arg's dad perched on a ledge just high enough off the ground to be out of harm's way. His arm hung down, waiting for Arg. A dozen saltopuses were snapping at Arg's heels as he sprinted between two Nn-Grrrdy and leapt over the fire pit. He raced to the cliff and leapt.

Arg's dad caught his arm and hauled him onto the ledge.

Below, the clearing quickly turned into a battleground. The Nn-Grrrdy speared one saltopus after another. Bodies soon littered the ground. But the saltopuses kept coming.

They chomped off Nn-Grrrdy toes. Ripped strips off Nn-Grrrdy legs.

And tore chunks out of Nn-Grrrdy bums. In the end there was only one thing the Nn-Grrrdy could do. With cries of pain and fear, they dropped everything and ran for their lives, chased by the saltopuses.

When the last Nn-Grrrdy cries faded, Arg's tribe
climbed back down. While the women gathered up
all the saltopus carcasses, the men piled the fire high.
Tonight they would feast.

94

Then they drank the rest of the fermented cycad sap. They now had plenty of fine flint stones for hunting and fire-starting. And they still had all their mammoth hides. What a great day!

Arg wasn't quite so sure if it was a great day or not. Where did that mystery cave boy come from? And what was he doing keeping all those saltopuses trapped in a cavern? It wasn't a very nice thing to do. In fact, it sounded just like something Hng would do.

A cold shudder raced up Arg's spine. Imagine if Hng and the cave-boy ever met. That would be too terrible to think about. Hopefully, Arg would never see the cave boy again.